Is Apatosaurus Okay?

by Ben Nussbaum

Illustrated by Trevor Reaveley

SMITHSONIAN INSTITUTION

To Rebecca and Larry and their new family member—B.N.

Published by Soundprints Division of Trudy Corporation, Norwalk, Connecticut.

Book design: Marcin D. Pilchowski
Book layout: Konrad Krukowski
Illustration studio: Artful Doodlers
Pencil illustrations: Chris Hahner

First Edition 2005
10 9 8 7 6 5 4 3 2 1
Printed in China

Acknowledgements:
    Our very special thanks to Dr. Brett-Surman of the Smithsonian Institution's National Museum of Natural History.
    Soundprints would also like to thank Ellen Nanney and Katie Mann of the Smithsonian Institution's Office of Product Development and Licensing for their help in the creation of this book.

Library of Congress Cataloging-in-Publication Data is on file with the publisher and the Library of Congress.

A Note to the Reader: Throughout this story you will see words in *italic letters*. This is the proper scientific way to print the name of a specific dinosaur.

IS APATOSAURUS OKAY?

by Ben Nussbaum

Illustrated by Trevor Reaveley

Soundprints

Where Children Discover...

An *Apatosaurus* lumbers toward a stream. Her heavy feet sink into the damp ground with a loud squish. *Apatosaurus* cannot go any closer. The marshy ground cannot support her. She would sink into the earth and be stuck.

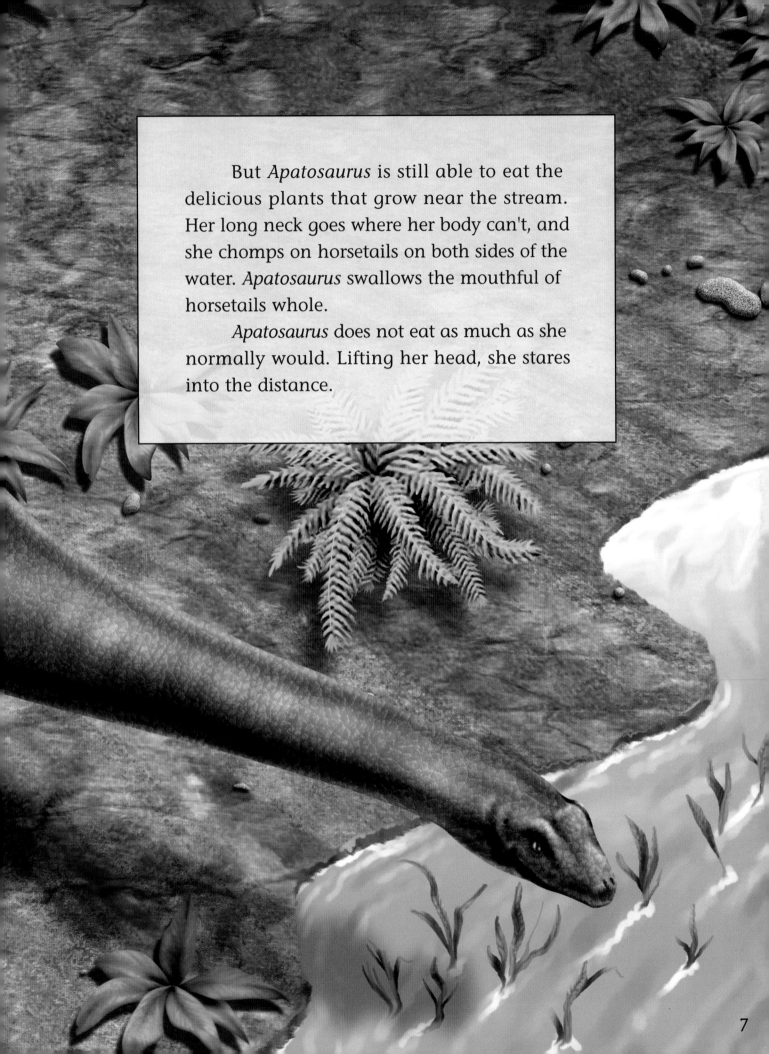

But *Apatosaurus* is still able to eat the delicious plants that grow near the stream. Her long neck goes where her body can't, and she chomps on horsetails on both sides of the water. *Apatosaurus* swallows the mouthful of horsetails whole.

Apatosaurus does not eat as much as she normally would. Lifting her head, she stares into the distance.

On the other side of the stream, *Apatosaurus* sees a group of *Brachiosaurus* and an *Allosaurus*. One *Allosaurus* by itself is not a threat to the group of *Brachiosaurus*, and the *Brachiosaurus* ignore the predator.

Apatosaurus watches the dinosaurs without moving. Something is making *Apatosaurus* very tired.

After backing away from the stream, *Apatosaurus* walks, even more slowly than normal, toward the edge of the forest. She reaches deep into the forest with her long neck, nibbling on the leafy cycad trees.

Apatosaurus cannot hear anything over the buzz of insects and the ripping sound she makes when she tears the leaves off the tree. She has let her guard down for a moment.

She doesn't know that she is being watched!

A pack of *Ceratosaurus* quietly approach *Apatosaurus*. The *Ceratosaurus* are hungry! *Apatosaurus* pulls her head back from the forest just in time to see the *Ceratosaurus* surround her.

Even when they are working together, *Ceratosaurus* would not normally attack a huge dinosaur like *Apatosaurus*. But they see that *Apatosaurus* is isolated from her herd right now. They can tell that *Apatosaurus* is moving slowly and is not as strong as she normally is.

Suddenly, the *Ceratosaurus* pounce! *Apatosaurus* whips her tail at the dinosaurs, knocking one over. *Apatosaurus* turns in the other direction, whipping her tail at the other *Ceratosaurus*. Her tail is a mighty weapon!

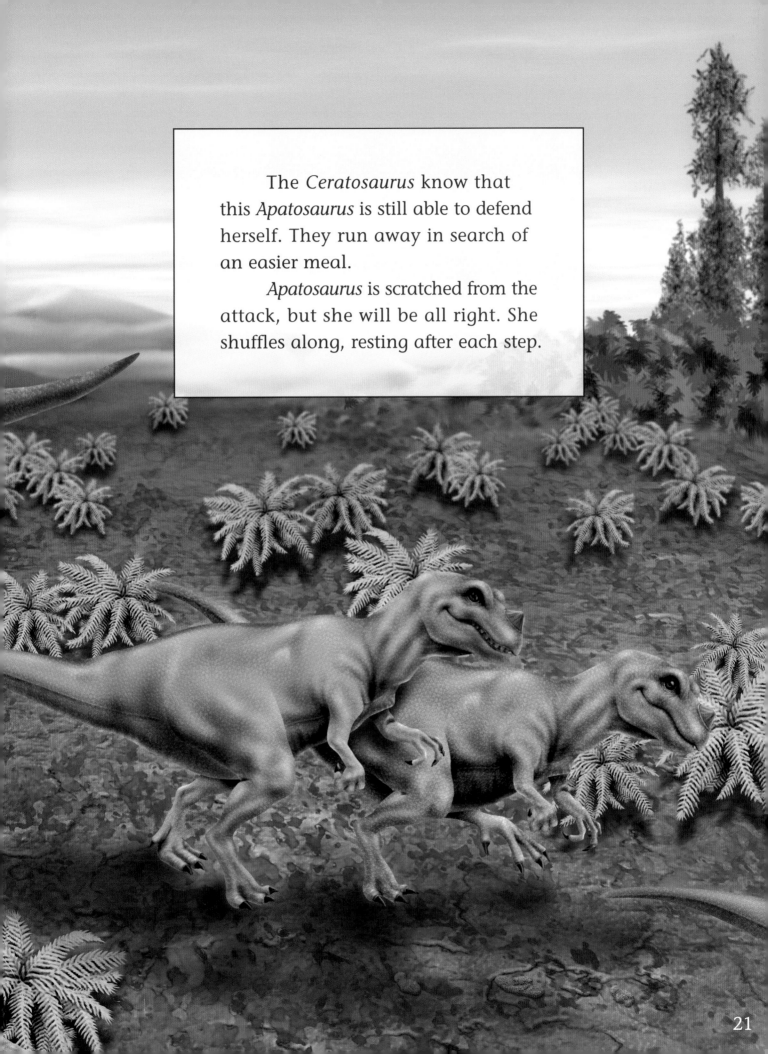

The *Ceratosaurus* know that this *Apatosaurus* is still able to defend herself. They run away in search of an easier meal.

Apatosaurus is scratched from the attack, but she will be all right. She shuffles along, resting after each step.

Apatosaurus stands still. She has found the place where she wants to stop. It is a nest that she built yesterday. After a while, she lowers her legs and tail close to the ground. A gigantic egg appears! *Apatosaurus* continues to lay eggs. She lays twelve eggs in all.

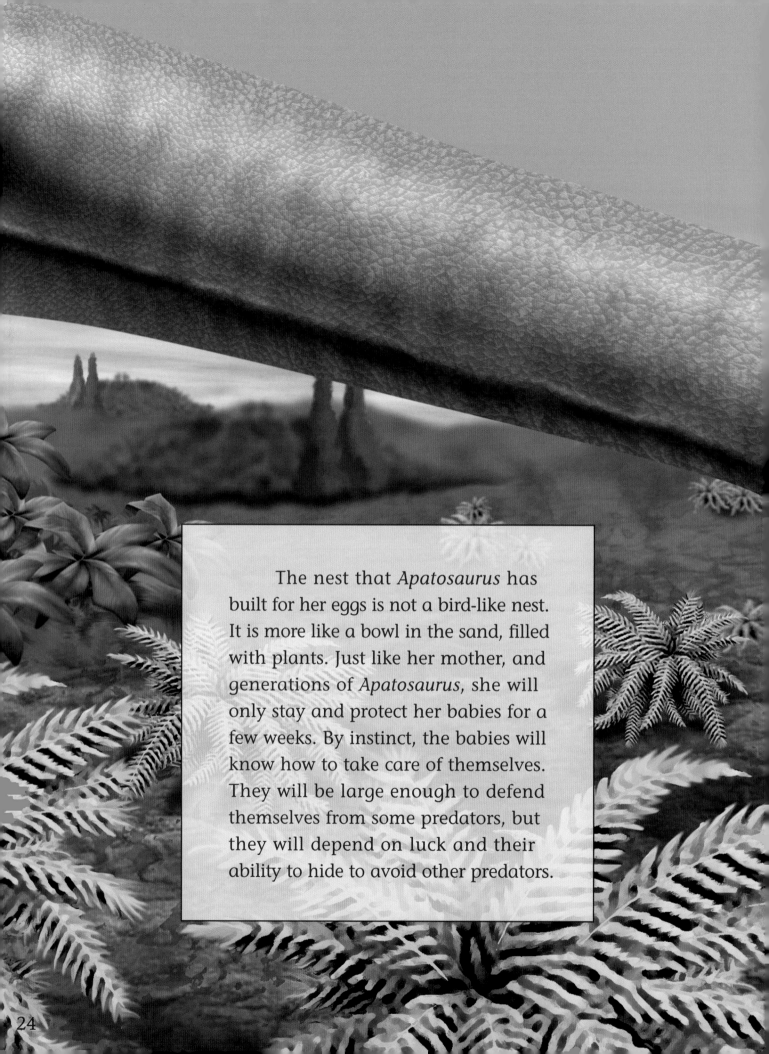

The nest that *Apatosaurus* has built for her eggs is not a bird-like nest. It is more like a bowl in the sand, filled with plants. Just like her mother, and generations of *Apatosaurus*, she will only stay and protect her babies for a few weeks. By instinct, the babies will know how to take care of themselves. They will be large enough to defend themselves from some predators, but they will depend on luck and their ability to hide to avoid other predators.

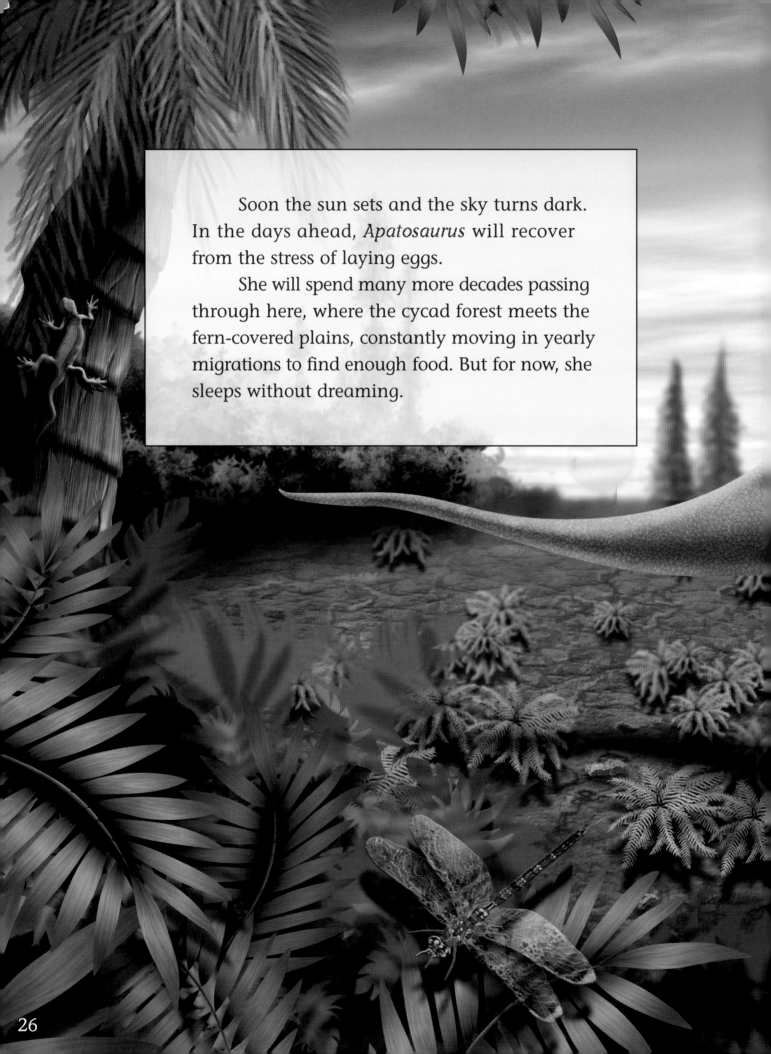

Soon the sun sets and the sky turns dark. In the days ahead, *Apatosaurus* will recover from the stress of laying eggs.

She will spend many more decades passing through here, where the cycad forest meets the fern-covered plains, constantly moving in yearly migrations to find enough food. But for now, she sleeps without dreaming.

ABOUT THE APATOSAURUS
(a-PAT-oh-SAW-rus)

Apatosaurus lived on earth about 150 million years ago, in a time known as the Jurassic period. *Apatosaurus*, which was once known as *Brontosaurus*, was one of the largest land animals to ever live. It weighed 30 to 40 tons. It stood as tall as a three-story building and was as long as a train car.

What made *Apatosaurus* so long was its neck and tail. Its neck alone was more than 20 feet long, and its tail even longer at over 30 feet. This long neck allowed *Apatosaurus* to poke its head into a forest to eat leaves from the trees. *Apatosaurus* used its long tail to defend itself.

But as big as *Apatosaurus* was, its head was less than two feet long. This meant that *Apatosaurus* had a very small brain, about the size of a large apple.

Apatosaurus had a long life for a dinosaur. It is estimated that *Apatosaurus* lived an average of 50 years!